THE VOICE IN THE

CLOSET

The Spite Lane Hauntings: Book One

by Christiane Erwin

LOST KEY
LITERARY

LOST KEY LITERARY, LLC

First e-book edition October 2023

First paperback edition October 2023

First audiobook edition October 2023

Cover art & interior by Christiane Erwin

Cover design by Christiane and David Erwin

ISBN: 979-8-9865426-3-8

ISBN (ebook): 979-8-9865426-2-1

More at www.christianeerwin.com

CONTENTS

PROLOGUE

Timmy Russell pulled the bed covers up over his tiny frame, tucking his quivering lower lip under the edge of the quilt. He hated it when his parents fought, and ever since they'd moved to 123 Spite Lane, his parents fought all the time.

"I can't believe you moved us here!" his mother yelled. "This neighborhood is awful!"

"You wanted a bigger house, I found us a bigger house!" his father spat in return.

Even though his bedroom door was closed, as was theirs, he could still hear them perfectly. There was a crash and the sound of breaking glass, probably one of the framed pictures his mother kept on her dresser. He told himself 6 years old was too old to cry, but tears filled his eyes anyway.

"Everyone here hates us!" his mother argued. "They're so mean!"

"Maybe you're just an unlikeable shrew!" Another crash, bigger this time. The lamp on her bedside table.

Timmy cuffed his ears with his hands, muffling the sound. He tried to imagine it was the sound of kids playing on the playground — not that anyone played on the playground in this neighborhood.

When they'd first moved to Lost Key, Florida over the summer, Timmy had walked down to the end of Spite Lane where his mother said he was sure to find other kids on the swings or slide. But the equipment was old and rusted out, and the grass overgrown, and Timmy felt like eyes were staring at him from the tall, piney woods that surrounded the area.

As he'd trudged home, the feeling had continued. He'd gazed up at the rows of tall Victorian houses with their gabled roofs and deep porches. Each house sat at odd angles high up off the street, beyond steep concrete steps, looming over passersby like a judgemental tribunal. His father said, when he'd visited before purchasing their house and moving the family from California, the neighborhood was bright and cheerful. Picture perfect. He'd described children running back and forth, riding bikes, and playing games. Timmy had seen nothing of the sort.

Timmy had no friends, and his parents had fought more and more since moving. He hated it here.

Slowly, he brought his hands down from his ears. Thank goodness, the fight seemed to have ended.

But there was another noise, something unfamiliar. It wasn't coming from the direction of his parents room — it was coming from up above.

Timmy cocked his head on his pillow. Was that a meow?

Timmy peered up at the wallpaper border that scrolled across the wall near his bedroom ceiling and studied the print. The paper was faded and peeling at the corners, but he could still make out images of a fluffy, black cat in a repeating pattern. In one panel, the cat sat prettily, it's black fur framing it's neck like a winter cowl. In another frame, it carefully cleaned its paw. It stretched. It yawned. It pranced with its tail held high. If Timmy stood in the center of the room and spun, the images of the cat would blur together and come to life like a movie on an old zoetrope.

He heard it again, a mewling cry. It had to be coming from the cat. Timmy squinted in the dark at the wallpaper border. It wasn't possible, was it? The sound couldn't possibly be real.

The image of the cat became clearer, and Timmy realized there was harsh, yellow light coming from under his closet door, gradually increasing in intensity, lighting up his room. He pushed himself up on his elbows and stared at the glow on the wood floor.

A shadow flitted as something inside his closet moved. Timmy's belly tingled at the sight. He didn't like this feeling. It reminded him of how he felt when kids at school told him scary stories about his house at lunchtime. They said his neighborhood was haunted.

The doorknob on his closet squealed slightly as it rotated, and the closet door began to open.

Timmy whimpered, "Hello?"

The door stopped midway. Timmy couldn't see inside, but he could hear someone — or something — breathing on the other side.

"Mommy?" Timmy asked, but he knew it wasn't her.

"Stay," a voice said breathily. It was the voice of a woman, gentle and kind. Something about the voice calmed him. It reminded him of his Aunt Trish, his mother's sister. In California, she had lived nearby. Whenever she babysat Timmy, she baked him oatmeal cookies. He could almost smell the cinnamon now.

"Stay with me... forever," the voice beckoned.

Could it be Aunt Trish? Could she want him to move back to his old home?

"Aunt Trish?" Timmy asked.

"Stay he-e-e-e-re."

It wasn't Aunt Trish. It couldn't be. The tickle in his belly turned cold.

"W-who are you?" he stammered.

"Sta-a-a-a-ay."

Timmy thought for a moment. Something told him the house itself was talking. It was the first time anyone here in Lost Key treated him like they wanted him around. Maybe, like Timmy, the house was lonely, too.

"I'm sorry. Mommy doesn't want to stay," he said quietly. "She doesn't like it here."

There was a rumble so low that it could not be heard, but Timmy felt it the way the floors at his old house would vibrate slightly when a train passed by in the night.

"Noooo," the voice whispered. "Stay."

A cold wisp of air tickled the back of his neck, and a flicker of movement caught his eye. He looked up at the wallpapcr border.

It couldn't be! The kitty had come to life! What was once a static pattern was now in motion. The fluffy cat was staring at him as it licked its paw.

Timmy blinked. He was too old to believe in Santa Claus, but young enough to think maybe, just maybe, there was a little magic in the world. He watched the cat with trepidatious fascination.

The cat stood, stretched, yawned, and began to walk from one side of the wall to the other. As it approached the closet, it looked back at Timmy, meowed, then leapt off of the wallpaper border and onto the top of the closet door. It meowed one more time, then hopped down into the closet, disappearing behind the door.

The boy sat all the way up in bed, straining to see against the glaring light. The cat reappeared, sauntering out of the closet and gracefully leaping up onto the foot of his bed.

Timmy's mouth opened into a thrilled smile. He had always wanted a cat! He reached forward to pet it, but it leaned away, ignoring Timmy's excitement.

"Come," called the voice in the closet. "Come... and stay forever-r-r...."

The cat hopped off the bed and headed back to the closet where it sat next to the opening and waited for the boy. He swung his legs out of the bed and slid onto the floor. His bare feet made a soft clapping sound as he landed and padded off towards the kitty.

"Come," the voice whispered as Timmy followed the cat into the closet.

"Kitty!" he squealed in delight, the sound of his footsteps fading into the bright void.

Once he was inside, no longer visible to the world of the living, the door closed. The light went out. And little Timmy was gone.

The next morning, Timmy's mom went to wake him for school only to find his bed empty.

"Timmy?" Mrs. Russell called as she looked under the bed, but he wasn't there either.

She went to the closet and was about to look inside when she heard a rustling sound overhead. She looked up towards the ceiling.

There, on the wallpaper border, was a bizarre likeness of her son in a repeating pattern. There was a likeness of him sitting cross-legged, laughing at something funny. Likenesses of him chasing a cat, sleeping in a curled up ball, and screaming in terror.

It wasn't possible.

It couldn't be.

Mrs. Russell shook her head in horror and disbelief. She felt a scream pushing its way up into her throat and slapped a hand over her mouth. Her husband, Timmy's father, was getting ready for work and she didn't want to startle him. He would only get angry.

She backed up slowly keeping an eye on the wallpaper, trying to understand, when one of the likenesses of her son, the one where he was sitting and laughing, came to life. He turned his head to look at his mother and cocked his head.

At that moment, all of the children on the wall came to life, turning to look at their mother, mocking her confusion.

In unison, they asked, "What's wrong, Mommy?" Their voices echoed throughout the room.

The scream finally escaped Mrs. Russell's lips.

She turned to run from the room, but the door slammed shut and the closet blasted open, emitting a harsh light that flashed brighter than the sun. Mrs. Russell jumped backwards at the sight, tripped, and fell with a thud to the floor.

Her sons yelled, "Mommy! Stay!" Their faces contorted in rage as they ran across the wall towards the closet. "STA-A-A-AY!"

Before she could crawl away, she heard Timmy's padded footsteps. He ran out of the closet and jumped onto his mother's belly. She hugged him hard in relief.

"Oh, Timmy! Thank God!" she exclaimed.

But her relief was cut short when another Timmy appeared. He sped from the closet and grabbed her bicep and smiled at her with sharp little teeth. Another Timmy ran out and grabbed her ankle. Another and another, carbon copies of her son kept showing up, their teeth were sharp and their eyes black and dead. They grabbed her pant leg, her waistline, her hair. They pulled as they chanted.

"Stay! Stay! Forever we stay! We promised not to go away!"

Mrs. Russell grasped at the floor, scraping the worn wood with her fingernails, but it was of no use. She disappeared into the strobing light, the closet door slammed shut, and the room fell silent — but only for a moment.

As Mr. Russell entered the hallway, ready to go to work, he heard Timmy's voice call out from his room.

"Daddy?"

What on earth? he thought. Usually his wife took care of the kid in the morning. He went to Timmy's room to see what was going on.

But he didn't see little Timmy or any sign of his wife — just a strange black cat sitting in front of the closet, and a yellow light glowing under the door.

Mr. Russell never made it to work.

A week later, a For Sale sign appeared in the yard.

ONE

Purple and orange lights violently flashed on and off, ghostly apparitions crawled across the dirty walls and ceiling, and a group of screaming girls ran frantically down a hall. Thirteen-year-old Mabel Mandal held her phone up to her nose, watching the trailer for Torture Town, Pensacola's premier Halloween haunted house, with a mixture of revulsion and excitement. She couldn't wait to go.

However, she and her friends faced a few challenges. For one, the tickets were an insane $65 a piece. More importantly, visitors had to be 16 or older to enter. Mabel wasn't sure she and her friends could pass, but she was willing to cake on however much make-up it took to try.

A text bubble appeared from her best friend, Archer Abel, partially blocking the Torture Town trailer.

SO WE NEED 65?! GIRL, THATS A TON OF $$$

Mabel replied, ACTUALLY WE NEED MORE THAN THAT. HOW MUCH DO FAKE IDs COST??

WTF?! IDK!!

Mabel sighed, opened an incognito window on her phone, and searched the phrase, "how to get a fake id."

Just then, the door to the bedroom burst open and an angry woman stormed in. It was Mrs. Grace, Mabel's neighbor and employer. She scowled at Mabel as she scooped baby Ben off the floor where he sat wailing so hard, his face was a deep, dark red and drool flowed like a waterfall down his chin.

Mabel had been so absorbed in her phone, she'd practically forgotten she was babysitting. How long had Ben been freaking out like that? Mabel hastily shoved her phone in her back pocket and popped up from her spot on the floor.

"Hi, Mrs. Grace. Has it been an hour already?" She feigned clueless innocence, tucking a lock of silky black hair behind one ear. Mrs. Grace wasn't buying it.

Mabel understood that it was her job to keep Ben happy, but, whatever, *nothing* made Ben happy. Mabel had rocked him and danced for him and jiggled his toys in front of him, but the kid could easily hear his concert pianist mother practicing down the hall. There was no way to keep him calm when he knew his mom was a few steps away and would come running if he just cried long and loud enough.

To prove the point, as soon as Mrs. Grace had Ben in her arms, the child quieted. He wrapped one chubby hand around his mother's shirt collar, stuffed his other hand in his mouth, and cooed softly.

Mrs. Grace sighed. "I couldn't concentrate with all the crying." She pulled a wad of cash out of her pocket and shoved it into Mabel's hand. "Here, just take it, and go home."

"Cool," Mabel said, cluelessly taking the money. She went to the door, then turned back. "See you Thursday?"

"I'll let you know," Mrs. Grace snapped, her voice cracking with tightly bottled frustration.

Mabel shrugged and left, walking through the house, out the front door, and across the street to her own home.

She stopped in front of the dilapidated two-story rental property to check their mailbox. No surprise — her mother hadn't checked it in days, so it was stuffed to the brim with mail. Mabel rifled through the junk. Plenty of bills and some coupons, but none for Torture Town. It figured — that place was surely too popular for discounts.

On her way to the side door, she passed the garbage can which was bursting with trash. She shoved the junk mail into the can while holding her breath to avoid the rank odor of rotting meat. Then she dragged the can down to the curb and headed inside.

"Sivaan! You forgot to take out the trash again!" she called as she entered the house, tossing the bills and coupons atop the kitchen table.

From far inside the recesses of the house wafted the sound of her 17-year-old brother's stereo blasting punk music. There was no way he had heard her. She jogged up the stairs and banged on his bedroom door.

"Sivaan! Open up!"

Her tall older brother, over six feet at 17-years-old, loomed over her as the door swung open. "Hey, Shivani. What's up?"

Mabel hated it when he used her real name. For one thing, she hated how it sounded too much like his name. For another, it reminded her of their dad — and he was no longer around.

"Ugh, it's *Mabel*, Sivaan," she protested. Mabel held out an open palm. "Also, I took out the trash for you. Pay up."

"What are you talking about?"

"You keep forgetting," Mabel said as she followed him into his room.

Sivaan turned down the music and flopped onto his bed with his phone, scrolling as he only half-listened to Mabel's plea.

"Mom pays you five bucks for your chores, right? I did it for you, so cough it up. Five bucks."

Sivaan zoomed in on something Mabel couldn't see and mumbled, "What do you need money for? You're just a kid."

"Am not!" Mabel insisted. "And none of your business."

Sivaan peered over his phone at her, squinting. "Do we need to have the sex-drugs-and-rock-and-roll talk?"

"Ew!" Mabel winced. "No, and I already know about that stuff anyway."

"Oh, yeah? What do you know? What's phrogging?"

"Phrogging has nothing to do with sex, drugs, or rock-and-roll, pimple butt."

Sivaan just laughed. He set down his phone on his messy bed covers. "Okay, fine, but if I'm giving you money, I need to know what you're going to spend it on. I don't want to be an accidental accomplice to a crime."

"It's for Halloween," Mabel said cagily.

"What are you dressing as this year?" he pressed.

"The cocaine bear," Mabel answered, and this much was true. She was planning to wear a bear costume and spread white grease paint around her nose.

Sivaan burst out laughing. "You better not wear that to school or they'll suspend you!"

Mabel crossed her arms. "That sounds better than going to class. Besides, what's the worst that could happen?"

"They'll tell mom," Sivaan said.

"What's she going to do? Punish me? It's not like she knows how to set a good example."

Sivaan's face fell. "Hey, be nice." With that, he rolled off the bed and went to his dresser where he opened a drawer and pulled a five dollar bill out from under some socks. He held it out to Mabel.

Mabel reached for it, but he snatched it back and gave her a more serious look.

"You can have this, but you have to promise me something."

Mabel folded her arms over her chest. "What?"

"Promise you won't use this to do something stupid."

Mabel crossed her fingers inside her armpit where Sivaan couldn't see. "Okay. Promise."

This time, he held out the money and didn't pull it away when Mabel went to grab it. She immediately turned to leave.

"Hey," Sivaan called when she reached the threshold. "Just so you know, Mom hasn't paid me to take out the trash in years."

Mabel sighed and mumbled under her breath as she walked away, "At least you used to get paid for your chores. Mom always made me work for free."

TWO

As soon as she was inside her room, Mabel shut the door. Unlike her older brother, Mable didn't keep her money in her sock drawer. She didn't even have a sock drawer — it was more like she had a clothes shelf.

When her dresser had broken years earlier, her mother had never replaced it. Mabel guessed this was because large pieces of furniture were difficult for her mother to steal. When Katie Mandal had brought home a plastic-wrapped package of foldable, cloth storage boxes, Mabel assumed her mother had lifted them off the shelves at Target. Or maybe she'd ordered them online and then issued a chargeback on her credit card, a trick she'd demonstrated to Mabel when she was just 5-years-old.

Mabel thought about her mother's kleptomania every time she used the boxes, and she didn't like to think about it, so she tossed things in the boxes she rarely needed and kept her clean clothes on a bookshelf instead.

Because her mother had a problem with taking things that weren't hers, Mabel kept her money in the safest place she could think of: the false bottom of an empty piggy bank. Mabel had figured out this one simple trick thanks to the help of her friend Fernanda. That girl was always coming up with clever inventions.

Mabel popped the false bottom off of the smiling pig and pulled out a wad of cash. She added the fiver from Sivaan and the ten from Mrs. Grace to a bundle of ones — she had forty-two dollars total. Mabel was scheduled to watch baby Ben every Tuesday and Thursday — that was three $10 sessions left before Halloween — so, thirty dollars plus forty-two. It would be enough for one ticket to Torture Town with $7 left over.

Mabel folded up the money and placed it back in the piggy bank's false bottom. Then she whipped her phone out of her back pocket and started over where she'd left off.

There was no set amount for the cost of a fake driver's license, but from what Mabel could gather, she could expect to spend around a hundred bucks. She whistled. That was ten hours' worth of babysitting gigs. Mabel turned off her phone and set it on her bookshelf.

Ten hours... Maybe Mabel could convince Mrs. Grace to take her wife on a very long date night.

And what about her friends? Mabel's friend group consisted of Archer Abel, Fernanda Flores, and Suki Saito. None of them was rich. She wondered if they would have enough money to go. If not, Mabel was determined to help them out any way she could.

Mabel burst out of her room, set to cross the street and ask Mrs. Grace for more jobs, or at least a few referrals, when she stopped in her tracks halfway down the stairs and pulled back, hiding in the shadows.

At the bottom of the stairs, Sivaan stood in the front doorway, his body blocking the person standing outside. Mabel recognized the voice. It was Mrs. Grace. And she didn't sound happy.

"Tell your mother I'm sorry," Mrs. Grace was saying, "but I just can't have Mabel over to sit Ben anymore. She just — she isn't cut out for childcare."

"I understand," Sivaan said.

"I know your family has fallen on hard times since your father passed," Mrs. Grace continued. "Arjun was such a wonderful man. It's just awful what happened. And Sara and I want to help, we really do, but—"

"It's okay," Sivaan insisted, cutting her off. Mabel knew he hated these platitudes from adults as much as she did. "I'll let my mom know."

"Tell Katie I said hello, and if she needs anything—"

"I will."

"How about you take this?"

Mabel couldn't see what Mrs. Grace was offering, but she knew. It was food and money.

"It's okay, really," Sivaan argued. "We're fine, Mrs. Grace. You don't have to keep bringing us things."

"It's no big deal. I made extra."

Sivaan grabbed whatever she handed him, something heavy, Mabel guessed soup. It was so patronizing, it filled her with rage.

They said their goodbyes, and Sivaan shut the door. Mabel practically jumped down the stairs. When she thudded onto the landing, Sivaan flinched so hard, he dropped the dark blue ceramic crock. It smashed on the tile entry floor and chunks of stew went flying. A mushy potato hit Mabel in the face.

"Mabel!" Sivaan yelled. "What the — that's not our pot! Now I'm going to have to get her a new one!" He walked through the mess towards the kitchen at the rear of the house, leaving puke-colored streaks on the floor as he went.

As he pulled a mop and bucket from the pantry, Mabel followed, grousing, "'Not cut out for child care?' Can you believe the nerve of that B?"

"Mabel, don't," Sivaan growled, filling the bucket with soapy water. "I don't have the energy for this right now."

"Do you think this means she doesn't want me to babysit on Thursday?"

"Of course, it means that!" Sivaan yelled. "Geez, Mabel, get a clue!"

"But I really need that money, Sivaan!"

"Well, maybe if you acted more maturely, you wouldn't have lost your job!"

Mabel's mouth fell open, but she didn't have a comeback at the ready. Sivaan shoved past her and went back to the entryway where he began to sop up the soup, forming a pile of chunky bits in the center of the room. She left him to finish the job.

Not cut out for child care. *As if*, she thought as she stomped up the stairs. Mabel was good with kids — baby Ben was the problem. He was smart, too smart for his own mom. Luckily, Mabel was smart, too.

Slamming her bedroom door behind her, Mabel stormed over to her laptop — actually one of her mom's old laptops. And her mom's Facebook account was still logged in to the old, sad social media website. Mabel immediately set about making a new business page. Category? Child care.

Then she went back to Google. *How do you make fake Facebook reviews?* Reddit results suggested it was possible — but the fastest, easiest way was to pay someone. Someone on a freelancing site was charging a buck per review. That seemed reasonable. Mabel figured she only needed five to ten reviews to make it seem like she was the best babysitter in the world.

I guess it really does take money to make money, Mabel thought. As she filled out the request form, she prayed her mom's saved credit card wasn't maxed out. She could always pay her back later.

THREE

Mabel ran into the lunchroom the next day and skidded to a halt in front of her friends, shouting, "You're not going to believe this!"

Mabel's best friends Archer, Fernanda, and Suki sat at the lunch table, eyes glued to their phones. Lunchtime was the only time the eighth graders were allowed to have their phones out, so their attention was a precious commodity. Mabel realized they weren't going to pay attention to her unless her announcement was especially good.

"We're going to Torture Town!" Mabel enticed, and suddenly she had everyone's attention.

"Wait, what?" Suki asked breathily in disbelief. She put down her phone and gazed at Mabel with giant onyx eyes behind enormous, round wireframe glasses. She pushed up the puffy sleeves of her peasant dress and rested her chin on them with dreamy anticipation.

"Girl, are you crazy?" Archer asked, one eyebrow cocked so high, it practically touched the thick ringlet of hair he had so meticulously styled over his dark brown forehead. "I thought tickets were, like, a million dollars." He pushed the ringlet away with multi-colored fingernails, but it fell right back down.

Fernanda didn't say anything, which was no surprise given her neurodivergence. Because she stared blankly at Mabel with hazel eyes, wore her hair parted in the middle and wrapped around her head in two identical braids that formed a perfectly symmetrical crown, and donned an embroidered blue shirt, to Mabel she looked like a Frida Kahlo painting.

"Tickets are only $65," Mabel said, taking a seat beside her friends and acting as though the price were no big deal.

"Whatever," Archer huffed, waving away the thought. "Can't afford it either way."

He turned a dramatic shoulder to Mabel and gave Suki an eyeroll, like, *Can you believe Mabel?*

Mabel opened up her lunchbox, pulled out her tiffin, and unlocked the metal compartments as she continued to explain.

"I got a job. And it pays good. Really good. If I play my cards right, I might be able to pay for all of you."

Suki fiddled with the chunky wooden bracelets wrapped around her wrists. "Okay, I'll bite. What job?"

Mabel gave her a sly grin as she pulled a lid from one of her containers, allowing the aroma of cinnamon and anise to escape. "It's a babysitting gig."

Suki and Archer groaned while Fernanda looked on.

"No, you don't understand," Mabel argued. "This isn't just any babysitting job. This one pays *thirty bucks an hour*."

"What?" Archer squeaked, dramatically throwing a hand up to his forehead as though he might faint.

"I know, right?!" Mabel laughed and began to chow down on her food.

Suki twirled the crystal that hung on a chain around her neck. "There's no way," she said in quiet disbelief. "That's more than I make when I do palm readings with my mom at the Lost Key Fall Festival, and our booth is always packed. Line out the door."

Mabel smiled with a full mouth and gave Suki a proud nod.

Fernanda spoke up. "I thought Mrs. Grace paid you ten dollars an hour?"

Mabel chewed and swallowed as everyone leaned forward to get the details. Mabel explained that, yes, Mrs. Grace paid ten an hour, but also Mrs. Grace had fired her (which was completely bogus), but *also* none of that mattered because Mabel had made a Facebook page with fake reviews to drum up more business — and she'd hit the jackpot almost immediately!

"This woman reached out and said she needs someone to watch her kid for two hours after school every day until she gets home, and she's willing to pay thirty dollars an hour!"

Suki mouthed the word "wow," but Archer folded his arms over his chest and frowned.

"Come on, honey, there's gotta be a catch," he argued.

"No catch," Mabel swore.

"I don't buy it. Is it, like, a possessed Exorcist baby?"

"No, just a 6-year-old little girl."

"And she, like, needs an exorcism? Her head spins around? She projectile vomits pea soup?"

"The mom says she will probably just sit and watch television the whole time."

Archer's eyes narrowed into little slits. "And where do they live?"

Mabel paused. She shoveled a huge bite of eggplant and rice into her mouth and spoke around it. "Spithe lame," she said unintelligibly, with bits of food flying out of her mouth.

"Come again?" Suki asked.

Mabel licked her lips, swallowed one more time. Her mouth went dry. "Spite Lane."

"Honey, no!" Archer shouted as everyone leaned back in surprise.

"Mabel! That place is haunted! You can't go there, you know that!" Suki admonished Mabel with a wagging finger.

Mabel shrugged as if she had never given it a second thought. "Y'all are making way too big a deal out of this. You know those stories are bogus."

"What stories?" Fernanda asked.

"Mabel, don't you believe in ghosts?" Suki rubbed her crystal, kissed it, and waved it around in the air. "Not that they require your belief."

Mabel rolled her eyes.

"Ghosts or no ghosts, that place is cursed AF," Archer said. "It's bad news. No one in their right mind would take a babysitting job there."

"Yeah, but, for THIRTY dollars an hour?!" Mabel argued.

"There's a reason they're paying that much, Mabel! And this close to Halloween...?" Archer made the sign of the cross over his forehead, chest, and shoulders.

Mabel licked her spoon. "Whatever. Y'all are crazy if you think I'm going to turn down that kind of money."

"What stories?" Fernanda asked again, slightly louder this time.

"Just think about it — TWO HOURS a day, every day after school — and there are eight days left before Halloween — that's $480!"

Archer chewed the inside of his cheek as Suki stared into space, calculating.

"Look," Mabel continued, "let's say it sucks and I hate it and the kid is a demon or whatever. I can just babysit for the 8 days, get my money, take you all to Torture Town, and never go back, right?"

Mabel opened one of the other metal containers, finding two dough balls floating in a sticky, sweet, brown syrup. She popped one in her mouth and chewed.

"If my math is correct, we only need $260 to buy four $65 tickets to Torture Town," said Archer.

"Your math is correct," Fernanda agreed.

"Right, so, what do you need all that money for, Mabel?"

Mabel licked her fingers and leaned over the table, lowering her voice. "Well, the age limit says 16 and up, so we're going to need fake IDs."

"Fake IDs?!" Suki screamed.

"Shhh! Geez, don't blow it," Mabel hushed her as she looked over their shoulders to make sure no one was listening. "They can get pretty expensive, but I did some research, and we can save a little money if Fernanda makes them for us. The extra money should cover supplies."

Without hesitation, Fernanda picked up her phone and began to search *how to make fake IDs*.

"Come on, y'all! Just imagine what we could do with fake IDs!" Mabel enticed. "Torture Town is just the beginning!"

"Girl, if you think anyone will believe we're 16…." Archer put his head in his hands and shook it.

"It's worth a try!" Mabel argued. "Suki is really good with make-up."

Suki shot them a coy smile with pink blushed cheeks that rounded like apples and straight, white teeth that glistened behind hot pink lip gloss. "It's true, I'm a great makeup artist, but don't forget my eyelashes are real, okay? You'll need falsies all the way."

"And, Asher, you have killer fashion sense."

Asher frowned again but said, "Thank yew."

"Come on! Ignore the stupid fake stories about Spite Lane and let's get scared for real at Torture Town!"

"What stories?" Fernanda demanded one last time as she set down her phone. "Also, Mabel, you owe me one-hundred-forty-two-dollars and sixty cents."

"What?"

"I ordered supplies to make the IDs."

Mabel, Archer and Suki looked at each other in disbelief.

"Already?" Suki asked.

"You have a credit card?" Mabel pressed.

"My parents gave me a savings account with a debit card attached for my birthday," Fernanda explained plainly. "It has a small stipend for my inventions."

"Well, well," Mabel said. "That could come in handy."

"I'll make the IDs, but you still haven't told me — what stories?"

Before Lost Key had become the bustling resort town Mabel and her friends knew it to be, it had been but a slip of sand that washed in and out of the estuary that divided Florida and Alabama. In the early part of the twentieth century, a hundred years before Mabel and her friends were born, few people dared build homes on that fickle ground. Sure, the Savage family had taken its chances, as had the McCrays, but the last bits of driftwood that had once been called "Beldame"

had finally washed away when Hurricane Ricardo rolled through in the fall of 2022.

No architecture was left of that era... except for a single strip of Victorian homes built by a developer named Gabriel Spitzer. After his home in nearby Lillian was lost to the Great Flood of 1919, he set out to try again. He took every penny he had left and put it into a sprawling estate on a pitch of mud on the northern side of Lost Key. His construction crew told him he was crazy — when it rained, the ground turned to quicksand — but Spitzer was determined to persevere. He told them to dig out the sand during the storms and had large fishing trawlers haul in stones that were used to build the ground back up again, essentially creating an island on top of the key.

Spitzer's Victorian mansion was built up so high on that pillar of stones and mud that, even when floods and hurricanes railed against it, the building prevailed. The eaves were tall and curved to redirect the angry wind, and the windows were narrow with heavy shutters that protected the thick, wavy panes of glass. When it easily weathered the squall of 1922 (which leveled most of the small towns around Pensacola and Mobile), families who had lost it all to the storm begged Spitzer to build something just as sturdy for them.

And so the development of the Spitzer neighborhood took shape. By the end of 1923, there were fifteen houses from gate to forest, each unique in design but built to the same exacting standards. To this day, the Spitzer mansion and the remaining houses stand, though they all show signs of wear and tear. The sign at the old iron gate, worn and never maintained, is now missing a few letters and reads as "Spite Lane."

This surprises no one as it is well believed across Lost Key that the entire neighborhood, once a bastion of modernity and strength, is violently haunted.

Some say Spitzer himself was the culprit. A strange man who some thought worshipped the devil, he was a recluse in his later years. He deeded the house to his estranged great-grandchildren when he died, and as far as anyone knows, it has remained empty ever since... although some say you can still catch a glimpse of Gabriel Spitzer in a suit and tie going for his nightly walk under the one streetlamp in service if you stay up late enough.

Others say the land was inhabited by a demonic, shape-shifting river monster since long before Spitzer arrived, and it was simply poor luck that the man thought he could claim what has always been and always will be the territory of someone — or something — else.

But the predominant legend has it that a group of teens decided to hold a seance in one of the houses for Halloween and unwittingly opened a gate between the dimensions, allowing an entity through that has not since left.

No one from Lost Key, no one with any familiarity with these stories, would ever willingly live on Spite Lane, but newcomers enticed by the homes' ample square footage and impossible-to-beat prices still come and go with regularity. Every once in a while, someone local and desperate seems to think they are immune to the darkness that resides there, and they take a job at one of the homes or date one of the residents or run an errand (just a quick one!) down the lane. It never ends well.

So, it stands to reason, that no babysitter in her right mind would ever take a job minding any of the Spite Lane children. No babysitter except for Mabel Mandal.

"So, now do you see why Mabel can't take this dumb job?" Archer said as he finished up his tale.

"Hm," Fernanda murmured, considering what she'd just been told. Then she nodded with certainty. "Yeah, sounds like a bad idea. I wouldn't do it, if I were you, Mabel."

Suki nodded conspiratorily.

"You gotta be kidding me!" Mabel spat as she gawked at Fernanda. "*You* believe in *ghosts*?"

"Nah," Ferndanda said without emotion. "I'm sure there's a logical explanation. Could just be confirmation bias."

"What's that?" Suki asked.

"When you fit an explanation to meet your pre-existing beliefs," Fernanda explained.

"Right," Mabel agreed. "Believing is seeing or whatever."

"So the rumors are probably not due to paranormal events," Fernanda explained. "But it could be a serial killer."

Mabel clapped her mouth shut and looked at Fernanda with wide eyes.

"Yeah," Fernanda said distantly. "Now that I think about it, definitely sounds like a serial killer."

The bell to end lunch rang, and the group of friends all jumped in their seats.

"Thanks," Mabel said sarcastically as she grabbed her things and stood to leave the table. "But serial killer or not, I'm definitely taking that babysitting job."

FOUR

An unmarked opening in the tall pines signaled the dirt entrance to Spite Lane. Sivaan pulled onto the shoulder of Blue Angel Parkway and put his car in park.

"I can't believe you took a babysitting job here, Mabel," he said to his baby sister. "What were you thinking?"

"I was thinking it was the 'mature' thing to do," she said, using his words against him. He just sighed.

Mabel leaned forward and peered out the car window through the dark canopy to try to see what lay beyond, but it was no use. The forest here had been allowed to grow unkempt for years, and the gate had been set too far back to see from the Parkway.

Mabel opened the passenger side door and hopped out.

"Wait for me at Badass Coffee after you're done," Sivaan instructed. "I'll swing by as soon as my shift is over."

Mabel nodded in agreement and closed the door. Then she turned to face the unmarked property and took a deep breath. She wasn't scared. It was just a stupid babysitting job. It was no big deal. Whatever. Behind her, Sivaan drove away.

It was then that Mabel realized the woman she was going to be working for mentioned a gate but not how to unlock it. Mabel pulled her phone out of her back pocket intending to text the woman for the code.

But as she approached the wood and iron structure she realized there was no need. The gate was open and in obvious disrepair. It likely hadn't closed in years. Studying it, Mabel wondered if it had ever worked properly. The proportions of the thing made no sense. It was taller on one side than the other, and broken lampposts jutted out awkwardly as though they had sunk unevenly into the ground. Mabel thought it was odd given how so much of the lore of the place was based on how sturdy everything had been built.

Beyond the gate, the dark tunnel of pines opened into a sprawling field littered with storybook houses built on sharply crested mounds. It was nothing like what Mabel had expected. Spite Lane wasn't exactly a lane, it was more like the winding path on a Candy Land board. The street curved back and forth so that the houses faced all angles, some with the rear facing another's front door. None of the homes had a proper yard. Few had a fence, and the fences that existed were all broken.

Accentuating the odd layout of the neighborhood were the houses themselves. Mabel had heard them called "Victorian," but this term must have been used loosely as the homes were all so unique. They each shared the tall, curved gables, the narrow turrets, and the deep, wraparound porches of the Spitzer mansion, but otherwise, the homes shared few architectural details. One had ornately carved wooden window frames, another had gargoyles monitoring the roof. Mabel walked past a house with such large, tattered cloth awnings, the whole thing looked like a pile of rags about to blow away in the breeze.

The houses were also painted a rainbow's worth of colors. There was an electric blue house with lime green trim, a house that was all purple including the roof shingles, and one house that was orange as a pumpkin with windows for eyes, a door for a nose, and broken porch rails that formed a mouth.

Double-checking, Mabel glanced at her phone for the Thomas's house number. As she recalled, it was 123 Spite

Lane. But this information was useless as the numbers of the homes made no sense.

The first one she'd passed was numbered 520. The second was 1633. Two of the houses didn't have numbers visible at all. It went without saying that the house farthest from the gate, and the largest, and the highest sitting, was surely the Spitzer house itself, so that wasn't it.

Mabel stopped in the middle of the quiet lane and began to type a message to her new employer asking which house was hers, when the dots began to bounce.

IT'S THE RED HOUSE WITH THE YELLOW FRONT DOOR, read the text from Ms. Thomas.

Mabel looked up. Did the woman know Mabel was standing right here in the street?

The red house was two houses (over?) (down?) (across from?) (the locations made no sense) away. Mabel walked right up to it with the distinct feeling Ms. Thomas was watching out the window, but when she knocked on the dingy wooden door, nothing happened. Mabel had to knock again before the woman finally appeared looking frazzled and out of sorts, not like she'd just sent a text. She was wearing a vintage-style apron over a brown floral print dress. Her shoes were black and clunky, and her mousy

brown hair was pulled up on top of her head in a messy bun
.

"Come in," she said, shooing Mabel inside like she was in a hurry, as she wiped her hands on the apron and walked through the living area to the kitchen.

As Mabel followed her across the room, she looked over to see a young tow-headed girl sitting on an overstuffed couch watching television. She had an empty ceramic plate on her lap and a half-empty glass of milk in one hand.

"I'll have more cookies right out!" cried Ms. Thomas. The girl did not look away from the teevee.

In the kitchen, the girl's mother donned a couple of oven mitts and pulled a tray of cookies out of the oven, placing them on the stovetop. Without waiting for them to cool, she yanked off the mitts, tossed them towards the sink, and began stacking the cookies on a plate. Without having a chance to cool, the cookies were too gooey to hold their shape. Ms. Thomas cursed as she stacked the crumbling sweets, wiping them off the spatula with a thumb and then licking said thumb when it burned.

Then she practically ran the cookies out to her daughter. Mabel had to step out of the way to keep from being barreled into by the woman, and in the livingroom she heard her say, "Here you go! Sorry that took so long! Fresh out of the oven!"

"They're broken," came the unexpectedly serious voice of the small child.

"I'm so sorry, Twyla," said Ms. Thomas. "I have to go, but I'll ask Mabel—"

"It's fine, just go," said the child quietly. Mabel was shocked at her impolite tone. If Mabel had ever talked to her mother that way, she would have felt the responding slap on her cheek for a week after.

More shocking was watching the woman re-enter the kitchen with fearstruck eyes. She had retrieved the other plate from the child and placed it on the counter. Then she sighed and seemed to calm a little.

Great, Mabel thought. *This kid is a real spoiled brat.*

That explained the high pay. Then she reminded herself that this gig was temporary. Take the money and run. Two weeks and almost five hundred bucks. Make it work.

"So, Mabel, right?" Ms. Thomas gathered herself, adjusting her messy bun and removing the apron. She threw it over a kitchen chair. "Thanks for coming. It's been really difficult to find someone because—" she stopped herself momentarily "— we just moved here recently. Anyway, thanks for being available on such short notice."

"No problem, Ms. Thomas," Mabel said.

"You can call me Kristy," said the woman.

No mother had ever suggested Mabel use their first name. It was kind of cool. It made Mabel feel grown up.

Mabel tried to guess Kristy's age. She seemed pretty young to be a mom. She didn't look much older than Sivaan. Mabel figured that's just how young moms were. They were cooler than the old moms who acted like they were so much better than Mabel, like they knew so much mo re.

"I won't be here when you arrive tomorrow. You'll meet Twyla at the gate where her bus drops her off after school at 3:30. Then you'll walk her home and hang out with her here till I get home from work at 5:30. I took the afternoon off today so I could show you around, but from here out, I won't be here, so —"

Kristy walked past Mabel again, went to the front door, and opened it. She pointed at something on the porch. Mabel followed to see. There was a small, metal box sitting on a table next to a broken porch swing.

"—there's a key in that box to open the front door. You can use that when you get here."

Mabel thought it was very strange that they would keep a housekey in such an obvious spot, but she just nodded. "Okay... Kristy." She said uncomfortably.

They headed back inside and stood in the entry looking over at Twyla.

"She can just watch television until I get home," said Kristy. "Make her a snack, whatever she wants. Play games. Draw. There are coloring books in the kitchen."

Without taking her eyes from the screen, Twyla put a finger over her lips and said, "Shhh."

Kristy bit her lip, then whispered, "Just don't go upstairs."

Mabel was caught off guard. "What?"

Kristy turned and gave Mabel a gravely serious look. "Whatever you do, just stay downstairs. Don't go up there, don't let Twy go up there. Stay down here until I get home. Do you understand?"

Mabel's curiousity was peaked beyond imagination. What on earth was upstairs?

"Mabel, promise," Kristy pressed. She put a hand on Mabel's shoulder. The weight of it was leaden. Kristy squeezed. "Promise me."

"Y-yes, of course," Mabel said. "We'll just hang out down here."

Kristy's fingernails dug under Mabel's collarbone. "Thank you."

Just as Mabel was about to cry out from the pain of Kristy's grip, Kristy let go. Mabel remembered Fernanda's warning about a serial killer. Could Kristy be a serial killer? Mabel imagined Kristy's eyes were what other people sometimes referred to as "crazy eyes." Was that enough of a sign to know for sure?

Kristy gave one last look at the 6-year-old, then yanked a purse from a hook next to the front door and slung it over her shoulder. "Great, okay, I'm going to the store. I'll be back by 5:30, like we discussed."

"Okay," Mabel said, the word barely out of her mouth as the swollen yellow door slammed shut.

Mabel heard a car engine rumble as Kristy slowly drove away. When she glanced back at the livingroom, little Twyla sat on the couch staring her down.

That's not creepy at all, Mabel thought.

In the background, the television droned on. A commercial Mabel had never seen advertised A COOL! NEW! TOY! It had been a minute since Mabel had played with toys. This one didn't look like something she would have ever owned or been interested in. It was an animatronic train with a face. Round eyes and round cheeks bulged over fat lips that opened to say catch phrases like, "Let's play a game!" and "Are you up for an adventure?" By pushing on the smokestack, two robotic arms popped out from the sides with cartoonish white-gloved hands, it cried out one of its pre-recorded messages, and it's wheels began to turn.

Mabel watched the child in the ad unbox the train, awkwardly hug it, and then follow it around their house as it rolled ahead, eyes darting back and forth, mouth opening and closing, hands jiggling on spindly arms, yelling out questions and commands.

Follow your demonic leader, she thought and gave a little laugh.

"What's so funny?" Twyla asked in monotone.

"Nothing," Mabel said. She took a step towards the kitchen. "Hey, want to color? Your mom said there are—"

"She's not my mom," Twyla said.

Mabel was caught off guard but tried not to show it. What was that supposed to mean?

"Oh, well, that's okay," she replied. "Anyway, she said there were coloring books in the kitchen."

Mabel passed by the child on her way to the kitchen and dining areas where she tried to guess which cabinet would hold the supplies. In the background, she heard Twyla switch the television off and assumed the girl would join her momentarily. Mabel rifled through a couple of cabinets by the kitchen door, shuffled the papers on the counter, and wandered to and fro, but she didn't find the books.

"Hey, Twyla, do you know where your mom — I mean, uh, Kristy — keeps the coloring books?"

There was no reply.

Mabel cocked an ear. The house was totally silent. She walked out to the livingroom. The teevee was off and the girl was nowhere in sight.

"Twyla?"

"Yes?"

Mabel spun. Twyla wasn't next to or behind her.

"Up here," said the girl.

Mabel looked up and saw Twyla at the top of the stairs.

Oh, no.

"Twyla! You're not supposed to be — can you come back down here, please? I don't think you should be up there!"

The young girl stood for a moment and observed Mabel as though she were legitimately considering her plea. She was perfectly still; her stringy hair hung as limp as her arms by her sides. Mabel could now see the shape of her dress. It hung loose over her skinny frame. All those cookies, and the girl looked like she hadn't eaten in weeks. She was so pale, she almost disappeared into the shadows of the upstairs hall, like a ghostly apparition of a child, not a real girl.

The girl opened her mouth to speak. "Why don't you come up here?"

And before Mabel could argue, the girl disappeared into one of the rooms.

FIVE

Mabel's heart began to thud so hard, she could feel her heartbeat throbbing all the way down to her toes. Her feet felt leaden, and her shoes were tight. Her brain was telling her to run up those stairs, grab the child (she couldn't weight very much, now could she?), and race her back downstairs. Whatever was up there, Kristy hadn't wanted her to see, and Mabel didn't want to see it either.

Her instincts kept her glued in place. There had to be some way to coax Twyla downstairs without having to go up there herself.

"Twyla, hey, how about you come back down here?" Mabel called as nicely as possible. She gripped the polished wood banister with both hands and squeezed. "Twyla? Twy?"

No answer.

"There are more cookies," she coaxed. "We can watch teevee together."

Silence.

"Twyla? I need you to come back downstairs. Upstairs is off-limits, okay? I'll play any game you want. Come on, anything you say, just come down!"

Mabel knew it would be of no use. She had seen how this kid treated Kristy. She was obviously used to getting her way. There would be no asking nicely. Ugh, what a disaster.

Mabel realized she had two options. Strike fear into the kid, or go up after her and drag her back down.

"Twyla, I'm going to need you to come back down here right this instant!" she shouted. "If you don't, I'll give you a spanking!"

A spanking?! Where on earth did that come from? Nobody spanked kids these days. Even Mabel's own parents had only done it once — maybe twice, Mabel could hardly remember. Besides, Mabel was just a babysitter, not a parent. She knew she had no right to touch somebody else's kid.

But she was also feeling desperate. Still no sight of or sound from Twyla. Mabel was going to have to go upstairs.

She took a deep breath and gathered her courage. Why wouldn't Ms. Thomas have wanted them to go upstairs?

There had to be a rational explanation, like it was messy or there were dangerous tools laying around or... Mabel couldn't think of anything else.

Actually, she could think of something — Kristy was a serial killer and the bodies of her victims were strewn about upstairs. Dead. Maybe alive. Mabel imagined severed body parts and people held like animals in cages begging to get out.

It couldn't be that. Twyla would have freaked by now.

Mabel put her foot on the first step. It creaked loudly as she put her weight onto it.

"Twyla, don't make me come up there!" she called out, but there was a shakiness to her voice. No hiding her own fear.

One foot after the other, Mabel climbed the stairs slower than a sloth crossing a busy road. She paused halfway up.

It would make more sense to go fast, she thought, *and grab the kid and run back downstairs without ever looking and seeing whatever it is Kristy didn't want me to see.*

She psyched herself up and was about to break into a sprint, taking the last few steps two by two, when she heard something that made her breath catch in her throat and the skin on the back of her skull tingle.

A voice.

Someone upstairs.

Someone whispering.

Mabel strained to hear. From beyond the doorway to the room Twyla had disappeared into came a voice, low and raspy.

"We can do it together," it said.

Then a reply — this time, clearly Twyla's voice. "Yes, together."

The low voice again: "We're running out of time."

"Yes," Twyla agreed. "No time at all."

"Are you up for an adventure?"

"Of course."

Mabel felt slightly nauseous. Was someone up there in that room with the little girl? She knew the right thing to do was keep her safe, even if Mabel herself was feeling scared.

She clenched her teeth and powered through her terror, expecting to burst through the doorway, grab the kid and run.

But when Mabel landed inside the room, what she found was not what she expected.

Twyla sat up in a twin bed, her legs under the bed covers, looking like a sweet character from a storybook. The only light in the room came from the closet. The closet door was half closed, casting a beam on the foot of Twyla's bed —

where a train toy sat facing her, speaking its characteristic catch phrases. As Mabel ran up, Twyla leaned forward and popped the train on its smokestack. She turned and looked at Mabel as the toy said, "Let's play a game."

The batteries must have been low, for the thing sounded odd, its recording gravely and garbled. Mabel sighed. It was just the toy, that was all. Not a person.

She looked around the room. No body parts. No cages. No one but Twyla and the toy. The curtains had been pulled closed, so the room was mostly dark, but Mabel saw nothing out of the ordinary. Just a little girl's room, somewhat bare, but with all of things anyone might expect. A dresser. A wire basket full of stuffed animals. A rug covered in toys and games. Whatever Ms. Thomas hadn't wanted Mabel to see must have been in another room.

"Twyla, you scared me," said Mabel as she put her hands on her hips. "I think you know we're not supposed to be up here. Come on, let's go back downstairs."

Twyla didn't move.

"You can bring the toy, if that's what you came up here for. Just — let's go."

Twyla looked at the train, considering. "His name is Lazybones."

"Great, yeah, bring 'ol Mr. Lazybones downstairs."

"His name isn't Mister," Twyla said with a hint of frustration. "He likes it when I call him Bones." She grinned at the toy.

"Yeah, cool, whatever, just, come on now."

Twyla picked up the toy and held him in her arms, stared lovingly into his face. Mabel's eyes, on the other hand, wandered around the room and up the wall and eventually landed on the wallpaper border that sat against the ceiling.

She had to do a double-take when she realized what was printed on the faded paper.

The wallpaper border was designed in panels that repeated over and over, a sequence of scenes featuring a middle-aged man doing inexplicable things. In one scene, he was crawling on all fours. In another, he was running while looking over his shoulder. He was on his knees, begging at the sky. He held his face in his hands in despair. In every scene, he looked scared out of his mind.

"What the he—" Mabel stopped herself before cursing in front of the child.

"What?" Twyla asked, curious.

"That's messed up," Mabel said, pointing to the wallpaper. "Doesn't that creep you out?"

The girl shrugged. "I kinda like it."

"Seriously?"

Twyla giggled as she slid out of bed, the train toy still in her arms. "We can go downstairs. I want more cookies."

Mabel sighed. Finally. She went towards the closet door, intending to turn off the light, when the girl shrieked.

"NO!" she screamed. "I want it on! Keep the light on!"

Mabel stopped in her tracks.

"Fine," Mabel said. "Geez."

As if in response, the light inside the closet flickered.

Needs a new bulb, Mabel thought, but she didn't investigate. Without ever looking inside, Mabel followed Twyla down the stairs.

SIX

"So, then what happened?" Archer asked as he leaned across the table, hanging on Mabel's every word despite the clamor of the middle school lunchroom around them.

"That was it," Mabel answered. She unlocked her tiffin and inhaled the aroma of curry with chickpeas, Sivaan's specialty. "We ate cookies and watched some cartoons and then I walked down to a coffee shop where I waited for Sivaan to pick me up." Mabel stirred the curry, half-wondering what she was going to do when he eventually moved out and went to college. Maybe he could teach her how to cook.

"You're not going back, are you?" Archer asked.

"Of course, I am," Mabel said, rolling her eyes and taking a bite of her food.

Suki gasped. "Don't do it! I asked the cards last night about your babysitting job, and I pulled the Knight of Swords!"

"I don't know what that means," Mabel said around cheeks stuffed full of rice and curry.

"It means you're in danger, obviously!" Suki whined as though Mabel was being dense on purpose. "You're playing with fire, girl. Tsk, tsk, tsk." The bangles around Suki's wrists clinked as she waved her finger back and forth.

"I agree with Suki," Archer said. "You don't need Tarot to tell you the obvious. Something bad is going on in that house." He tugged on his starched purple shirt sleeves with an air of authority. Archer liked to dress up like a fashionable morning show host — and Mabel agreed that he would be famous someday.

"It's not like anything weird happened," Mabel argued. "I went upstairs and it was just a regular upstairs. No dead bodies anywhere. I don't even know what Kristy — that's what she said I should call her — was so worried about."

Mabel left out the part about the strange wallpaper border. That, she figured, was just a weird decorative choice.

"Did you look in *every* room upstairs?" Archer countered.

"No, but that's not the point. I mean, if she doesn't want us to hang out up there, that's fine, we won't." Mabel put down her spoon and reached into her backpack. "Besides, check this out!" She pulled out a wad of twenties. "Sixty dollars!"

Without hesitation, Fernanda plucked the cash from Mabel's fist. "You still owe me $82.60."

"Fernanda! Are you effing kidding me right now?"

Fernanda didn't usually make jokes. She deadpanned, "No," and put the money in her own backpack.

Mabel sighed. "Fine, I'll be earning way more than that anyway, and Torture Town is gonna be so worth it. But you better have exact change for me in a couple of days."

Fernanda chomped a bite out of her jelly sandwich and shrugged in agreement.

The next two babysitting visits on Thursday and Friday went without a hitch. Sivaan dropped Mabel off at the entrance to Spite Lane. Mabel waited for Twyla's bus to show up. She walked Twyla home, and she made snacks for them to eat while they watched teevee. Since the first day Mabel had babysat, Twyla had not gone upstairs. Mabel thought it was turning out to be the easiest money-making venture in the world.

As they watched cartoons, Twyla kept her toy train, Bones, on the coffee table in front of the couch where he stared ominously at Mabel. Mabel tried not to think much of it. Kids had toys, and this one was just like all the others.

But Bones clearly needed a battery change. Every once in a while, he would murmur one of his catchphrases unprompted. It would whisper out of the speaker under his boiler. "Up.. for... adventure?" And without moving, his bug eyes would begin to swirl in their sockets. Mabel didn't love this part of their time together, but she was mostly able to ignore it.

Monday afternoon, however, after Mabel returned from their weekend break, Bones was in markedly worse shape. His arms wouldn't pop out, his lips gaped open, and his eyes had rolled all the way up and gotten stuck in that position. He looked positively ill.

"Let's... play... a game," Bones spontaneously rumbled.

Mabel couldn't take it anymore. While Twyla sat on the couch eating a plate of brownies covered in rainbow sprinkles, Mabel retreated to the kitchen to find a screwdriver and some batteries.

"Twy, do you know where y'all keep the tool chest?" Mabel called out to the little girl.

"No," Twyla said distractedly in return. Her favorite show was on, and she was difficult to interrupt, so Mabel went back to looking in every cabinet high and low before finally finding it.

Mabel returned to the couch and grabbed Bones, turning him upsidedown, looking for the battery compartment.

"Hey!" Twyla cried. "What are you doing?" She jumped up and viciously grabbed Bones out of Twyla's hands.

"Chill out," Mabel said. "I was just going to give him new batteries so he'll talk like a normal toy again."

"He is normal," Twyla argued. "There's nothing wrong with him." She hugged the hard plastic toy to her chest as though he were a security blanket.

"Totally cool, totally cool." Mabel put up her hands as though she'd been caught mid-crime. "We don't have to fix him if you don't want to."

She set the screwdriver down on the table and took her seat on the couch. Next to her, Twyla clutched the the toy so that it faced Mabel. She could feel its unnaturally round eyes staring her down. She wondered if she could find a way to sneak some new batteries into him when Twyla wasn't looking. Better yet, maybe she could hide him and Twyla would forget about him so they could watch cartoons in peace.

But Twyla and Bones never left the edge of Mabel's peripheral vision. It was as though they were silently awaiting her next move.

Bones was nowhere in sight when Mabel and Twyla entered the house on Tuesday. She was eager to get a break from the broken toy, but she was equally bored of cartoons.

"Hey, Twyla," Mabel called as the girl went straight for the remote, "I couldn't help but notice that no one in your neighborhood seems to decorate for Halloween."

Twyla paused with her finger on the ON button. She watched Mabel without turning on the television set.

"We should do something to decorate, dontcha think? We could draw pumpkins and put them in the window or make a construction paper garland."

Mabel said this as she crossed to the kitchen, hoping the little girl would follow. In the cabinet, Mabel found the supplies and set them out on the table. A moment later, the girl stood watching her from the door.

"Come on," Mabel coaxed. She took a seat in one of the kitchen chairs. She'd found a bucket with old, broken crayons, glue sticks, and safety scissors. "What do you want to make?"

Twyla didn't answer, but she did cross to the table and sit down.

Certainly, she's made arts and crafts at school, right? Mabel thought. *Poor kid looks like she's never seen a crayon before.*

Mabel folded a piece of orange construction paper in half, opened it up and laid it flat on the table, and, using the crease as a center line, began to draw a jack-o-lantern on one side. Then, using the scissors, she folded it up again and began to cut out the pumpkin along the lines through both sides of the paper so it would make a symmetrical design. When she was finished cutting, she opened it up and showed Twyla the face by sticking her tongue through the jagged mouth.

Twyla laughed. It was the first time Mabel had seen her show joy.

"I like you," Twyla said.

Mabel blushed. "Thanks. I like you, too."

"You're nicer than Kristy," Twyla said, licking her lips. "I wish you lived here."

Mabel wasn't sure what to say. "You do?"

Twyla nodded. "I wish you didn't go home and you stayed here all the time."

Mabel put down the drawing and started working on another pumpkin. "That's sweet. Wanna make one all by yourself?" She held out the folded paper to Twyla, but the little girl didn't drop her gaze. She stared Mabel directly in the eye.

"You should stay."

Mabel cleared her throat. "Thanks, but I think my brother would miss me. And your mom probably wouldn't like it much if I never left, either."

"I told you, she's not my mom."

Mabel frowned. She had forgotten, but, yeah, Twyla had mentioned that.

"Well, then, your sister wouldn't —"

"Kristy's not my sister. She's my dad's—" Twyla cut herself off.

At this point, Mabel thought she understood. "Your dad's girlfriend?" she suggested. Twyla didn't respond.

Maybe Kristy was his wife; Twyla's stepmom. Either way, Mabel could understand why Twyla might treat her badly. Maybe her parents had divorced or, worse yet, her mother had died, and she blamed Kristy. That could also explain why Kristy did so much bending over backwards to please the little kid.

It didn't, however, explain *where* Twyla's father was. Mabel hadn't met him, and Kristy had never even mentioned him.

"Your dad must work a lot," Mabel said, fishing. "I never see him around. Does he... come home late?"

Twyla's lips stiffened into a tight line.

Careful, Mabel, Mabel thought to herself. *Tread lightly.*

"You know, I haven't seen my dad in a long time," Mabel offered. "And my mom isn't around much either. It can be pretty lonely, not getting to see your parents very often. Do you ever... feel lonely?"

Twyla's face grew beet red. Mabel knew she was on thin ice, but her curiosity was piqued.

"Hey," she said quietly, reaching a hand out across the table. "We don't have to talk about it if you don't want to, okay? But if you ever want to talk, I'm here."

She was about to give Twyla's hand a squeeze when the little girl balled her hand into a fist and pulled it away.

You pushed it too far, Mabel thought. *Give her a minute to cool off.*

Gathering the crayons and scissors, Mabel slid them across the table towards the girl. Then she stood up.

"I have to go to the bathroom," she said. She figured a few minutes alone with the crafting supplies might be good for Twyla. As she started to walk away, she internally congratulated herself for how she handled things and even though maybe she should be a child psychologist one day.

Then Twyla spoke.

"I get to see my dad all the time," the girl said. "I can see him whenever I want."

Mabel looked back at her, more confused than ever.

"Oh. Well, that's great," she said. "I'll be right back."

Mabel went to the bathroom. It only took a couple of minutes. But when she returned... Twyla was gone.

SEVEN

Mabel looked under the kitchen table and behind the counter. Twyla was no where to be found.

Crap, Mabel thought, running out into the livingroom. The television was off, and the girl was not on the couch or in any of the chairs.

Mabel passed the stairs and the bathroom. She peeked into the study on the far side of the front entry. The glass french doors were mostly closed. Mabel looked behind them, then under the ornate wooden desk. She peered through the window out onto the veranda and front yard. No sign of Twyla anywhere.

Crap, crap, crap!

Mabel went to stand at the foot of the stairs. She paused, listening. There was only one place the girl could be. She looked up.

"There's no time to waste," said a low voice.

Bones. That stupid train. Mabel should have known, if it wasn't on the coffee table, it was probably in Twyla's room.

Just like the time before, Mabel figured this would be easy. Retrieve the girl and the toy. Bring them both downstairs. There was no reason to think anything bad would happen when nothing bad had happened before. Just run up, grab them, and run back down. And then change the dang batteries in that thing. It sounded creepier than ever.

Mabel counted down (three, two, one!) and leapt from stair to stair, pulling herself up by the bannister as she went. She landed in the doorway to Twyla's room and found her same as before, sitting in her bed, the covers draped over her lap.

But this time, Bones was not sitting across from her.

Twyla silently observed Mabel. Mabel scanned the room, confused. Where was the toy? She knew she had heard it talking. The closet door was closed, and the room was dim. There were toys scattered about, but none was the talking train.

"Twyla? Where's Bones?" Mabel asked, taking a step into the room and looking around.

Twyla, in characteristic fashion, didn't answer the question. Instead, she said, "Kristy doesn't like it here."

Mabel scratched her head. "Oh? Okay, well, I know sometimes the things grown-ups say to kids don't always make sense, but, ah, we're still supposed to follow their rules, so why don't we head back downstairs?" She got on her hands and knees to look under the bed. Still no sign of the animatronic engine.

"Kristy hates this house, but I like it," Twyla went on. "I don't ever want to leave."

"Right. Okay. Yeah. How about we just find Bones, and—"

"I told Daddy I didn't want to leave, but he said Kristy was my new mom, and if Kristy wanted to move, we'd have to move."

"Do you know where Bones is?" Mabel looked behind the bedroom door. Nothing.

"I didn't want Kristy to be my mom. I told the house I hate Kristy. So, the house told me a secret that would make everything okay."

"Where was the last place — wait, what?" Mabel stopped scanning the room for the toy and looked at the little girl in surprise.

"Now we're never moving."

Mabel's stomach flopped up into her chest.

"Me and Daddy are going to live here forever."

Bile shot up into Mabel's throat. Was it possible for a serial killer to be just 6-years-old?

"Twyla," Mabel said quietly, "we have to go downstairs now. I mean it."

"I like you, Mabel. And the house likes you. It wants you to live here forever, too." The girl gave Mabel a sickly smile.

Mabel caught a glimpse of something moving out of the corner of her eye, something high up, near the ceiling. She glanced at the wallpaper border. The images were shrouded in shadow, but the movement was unmistakable. The man she'd seen days before in an odd, repeated pattern was no longer afraid or upset. He was looking directly at Mabel, nodding in agreement with the girl.

But that was impossible.

Mabel couldn't breathe. She tried to inhale, but her lungs were frozen, her chest unable to expand. She made a squeaky gurgling noise. Twyla's smile grew.

"Stay with us, Mabel," the men on the wall called to her. "Stay here with us — forever."

Mabel realized there was a yellow light emanating from under the closed closet door, growing in intensity. The doorknob squeaked as it turned on its own. The closet door slowly began to open. Mabel took one step backward, then another, knowing she should grab the kid and run but unable to make herself do it.

"Sta-a-a-ay," the men whispered, and as they did so, Mabel heard the familiar squeak of toy wheels turning. Bones rolled slowly out of the closet, his eyes turning round and round in his head. The train turned to face her and continued towards her. It reached out it's spindly arms and gloved hands.

Behind Bones, a hand appeared — a man's hands. It grasped the side of the door. A polished loafer poked out of the closet, then salt-and-pepper gray hair, then a forehead, then cloudy gray eyes. Already, Mabel could tell it was the man from the wallpaper border.

But before he could emerge completely, Mabel turned and ran.

She leapt down the hall, jumped over the first set of stairs onto the landing, then jumped down the last half, pounding the floor so hard, it hurt her heels. She opened the front door and burst onto the veranda — only to run smack into Kristy Thomas. They toppled into a pile of arms and legs.

"Mabel?" Ms. Thomas wheezed. "What happened?"

She grabbed Mabel's arm and helped lift them to a stand.

Mabel had no idea how to answer. The look on Ms. Thomas's face said she didn't have to. The woman looked through the open door at the staircase. Then she looked back at the babysitting teen.

"I think Twyla — we — I didn't mean to —" Mabel couldn't find the words.

Ms. Thomas looked angry. "Please, no. Tell me you didn't go upstairs." The woman appeared ready to sprint up there and see for herself.

They were both shocked to see Twyla padding down the staircase with Bones in her arms.

The three of them stood at the opening to the house, staring back and forth at one another.

"Twyla," Ms. Thomas said with obvious surprise. Mabel wondered what Kristy Thomas had expected. Did she know what was going on with the closet upstairs?

"I thought I lost Bones," Twyla said with a smile. "But I found him. Everything's better now."

"I see," said Ms. Thomas, and she looked to Mabel for confirmation. "Well, I guess I'm glad everyone is doing okay."

Mabel forced her lips to turn up at the corners. She had no idea what to say.

"So, we'll see you tomorrow, Mabel?" asked Ms. Thomas. She pulled three folded-up twenties out of her purse, daring Mabel to take them and confirm she would return.

Mabel considered the money. She gingerly took it from the woman's fingers and nodded.

"You bet," the teen said. "Looking forward to it. See you then."

EIGHT

Wednesday at lunch, Mabel absentmindedly pushed her rice around in her tiffin as her friends talked Halloween costumes. She'd spent all day thinking about the previous afternoon. She paid no attention as Suki discussed dressing as Emily from *Corpse Bride*, but she couldn't afford a new wig, so she was planning to wear the Harley Quinn wig she'd bought a couple of years earlier.

"Do you think it will work?" Suki asked as she adjusted her oversized hoop earrings. "The wig has pigtails, but maybe I can figure out how to make it look like they're just, y'know, flowy hair or something."

"It will be fine," Archer said. He was conflicted about his own costume choice. He wanted to go as Ziggy Stardust, but he wasn't sure anyone would "get it."

"I don't get it," said Suki, as if on cue. "Who's Zigly Starters?"

"Ugh, seriously?" Archer groaned, rolling his eyes. "Mabel, you know who Ziggy Stardust is, right?"

Mabel didn't answer. She was stirring her food as though she were laboring over a witch's cauldron.

"Mabel? Earth to Mabel. Come in, Mabel."

Fernanda jabbed Mabel with an elbow. "Hey."

"What?" Mabel yelped, jumping. She accidentally flicked her fork, and her rice went flying.

"Jeez, Mabel, are you okay?" Archer jutted out his lower lip with mock concern.

"Of course," Mabel said, gathering her wits. "I'm fine. What's up?"

"Did something happen at the house on Spite Lane?" Suki asked. "You seem spooked today."

Suki and Archer looked at one another, this time with actual concern.

"No, no, nothing happened," Mabel lied. "I'm just tired. Babysitting is a lot of work."

Archer didn't seem convinced, but he accepted her answer. "So, how much money have you made so far?"

This question brought a smile to Mabel's face. "Almost two-hundred dollars."

"Whoa!" Suki was impressed. "Mabel, that's amazing! I can't believe how this all worked out!"

"For real, Mabel," Archer agreed. "I really didn't think I'd ever say this, but I gotta give it to you — you were right. Turns out Spite Lane isn't haunted, it's flush with cash!" They all laughed. "You still planning on taking all of us to Torture Town?"

Mabel forced a smile. She didn't want to go back to Spite Lane and had been trying to come up with a valid excuse all day, but she was so close to earning enough to take her friends to the haunted house.

She nodded and said, "You bet."

Her friends were overjoyed.

"This is very generous of you, Mabel. Thank you," said Fernanda.

Mabel was stunned. Fernanda spoke so little. It meant a lot that the girl would express her gratitude. Mabel leaned over and gave Fernanda a squeeze around the shoulder.

"My pleasure," Mabel said.

Fernanda squiggled uncomfortably out of Mabel's grasp.

"By the way, all of your fake IDs are ready," she said, changing the conversation. "And my mom offered to give us a ride."

"Ohmigod, but does your mom know about the age limit?" Suki put her hands to her cheeks in shock.

"No," Fernanda said. "She doesn't know."

"Phew!"

As her friends struck up a new conversation, this one about their hopes and expectations for the trek through Torture Town, Mabel's mind wandered off again. She couldn't get the images of the afternoon before out of her mind: the moving wallpaper, the possessed toy train, the man in the closet.

Who was that man? Was it Twyla's dad? Was he living in Twyla's closet? Did the wallpaper really move, or were they playing some kind of cruel trick on her? What did Twyla mean when she said the house told her a secret?

By the time the end of lunch bell rang, Mabel had no answers to these questions, and no excuses for staying home and ditching the babysitting gig.

After Mabel got home from school, she went straight to her room and dropped her things on the floor. Then she trudged to Sivaan's room to tell him she was ready to leave for Spite Lane whenever he was ready, but Sivaan wasn't there.

Instead she saw, on the far side of Sivaan's room, their mother, Katie rifling through Sivaan's dresser drawers.

"Mom?"

When she heard Mabel, Katie stood up straight and tucked something Mabel couldn't see into her back pocket.

"Hi, sweetheart! What are you doing home so early?"

Mabel peered at her mother in suspicion. "This isn't early — this is when I always get home."

"Oh," Katie said. "I guess you're looking for Sivaan, too?"

"Yeah, I need a ride."

"Where to?"

"I have a babysitting job."

"You need a ride to Mrs. Grace's house across the street?" Her mother asked, confused.

Mabel stiffened, her hands balling into little fists. "I don't work for Mrs. Grace anymore, Mom. Didn't Sivaan tell you?"

"No," Katie said, as she started to walk past Mabel towards the door. "That's too bad. Really cool you got a new job, though."

"It's a better job," Mabel justified defensively, still feeling stung by her termination. "Pays more than double."

At that, her mother spun around. Mabel pinched her lips closed. *Stupid*. She couldn't believe she'd just told her mom about the money.

Katie looked at Mabel the way a lion might look at an antelope drinking from a pond. "I'm so happy for you."

The words came out of her mother's mouth, but Mabel could see in Katie's eyes, she was calculating. Mabel was more grateful than ever for the false bottom in her piggy bank.

"Yeah, well, I gotta go," Mabel said, changing the subject. "Don't wanna be late."

"I'm sure Sivaan is around here somewhere."

Both of them began walking into the hall, down the stairs, and towards the kitchen, Mabel on her mother's heels. They found Sivaan in the kitchen, slurping down a mango lassi.

"Sivaan, I hear you're taking your sister to her babysitting job? That's so sweet," Mrs. Mandal said hurriedly as she gave Sivaan a quick peck on the cheek and kept walking. "You're a good brother."

She passed him and went through the kitchen to the mud room where she grabbed a jacket off the rack next to the back door. "I have to go to work. Back later. Sivaan, can you throw something together for dinner? Have fun, you two! Be good! Love you, bye!"

And with that, their mother was out the door.

"Work?" Mabel asked with suspicion.

Sivaan placed his glass in the sink and filled it with water. "She got a new job at a department store."

"Until she steals something and they catch her," Mabel said, scrunching her face in disgust.

"Alright, Mabel, that's enough. Let's go," Sivaan said. He grabbed his car keys off the kitchen table and headed out the door.

On the way to Spite Lane, all Mabel could think about was how she found her mom in Sivaan's room. She didn't see what Mrs. Mandal put in her pocket, but she didn't have to guess. Her mother had been rooting around in the same place Sivaan had gone to get Mabel a five dollar bill.

"Sivaan, I need to tell you something," Mabel said after giving it some thought. She knew it would break his heart, but she had to tell him what she saw.

"What is it?" Sivaan asked, not taking his eyes from the road.

Mabel sighed. "I saw something today, something bad. I went to your room to find you, but you weren't in there. I found Mom instead. She was—" Mabel swallowed as she drummed up the courage to tell Sivaan the truth "—she was stealing money from you, Sivaan. I don't know how much, but I saw her going through your drawer, the one where you keep your money. You should count it when you get home."

Sivaan was quiet. They slowed down for a stoplight, sped up when it turned green, and slowed for another red before he finally replied.

"I know, Mabel," he said quietly.

"What?"

"I know Mom takes money from my dresser."

"You know?!" Mabel was shocked beyond belief.

"Yeah," he said. "Actually, I put money on there on purpose. I meant for her to find it. If she took it, that's okay, Mabel, because I wanted her to."

Mabel had no idea what to say. She looked outside and watched as the gas stations and strip centers slid in and out of view. She wasn't sure what she was feeling, at first, but then the feeling became more clear. It was anger. Mabel was angry.

"Sivaan, why would you do that? Mom is stealing from you and you — you — you let her?"

"Yes."

"But, WHY?"

Sivaan slowed and pulled onto the shoulder. They had arrived at the darkened entrance to Spite Lane, the spot where the trees barely opened. Earlier, Mabel hadn't wanted to go back here. Now, she couldn't wait to get out of the car.

Sivaan put the car in park and turned to face Mabel. He slung an arm over the back of her seat, behind the head rest. His face looked tired and sad.

"I leave the money there because Mom needs it. It's hard for her — without Dad around."

"You mean it's hard for *all* of us because he *left* us!" Mabel yelled. "Don't act like it's not her fault. She's the one that made him leave by being a klepto."

Mabel fought back the urge to cry.

"Mabel, Mom didn't make him leave. That was his choice."

Mabel ignored Sivaan's excuses. "And then she told everyone he died just so she could get free money and food, like we were all some charity case."

"We *are* a charity case, Mabel. We can barely afford life without Dad's income."

"Maybe if Mom could just act more *mature*..." Mabel said mockingly.

"Besides, Dad might as well have died," Sivaan muttered. "It's not like we've heard from him since he bailed on us."

"Don't say that," Mabel sneered. "He's not dead. And if Mom would just stop stealing, he'd probably come back."

"It's not that simple," Sivaan said with an aching exhaustion in his voice. "Mom has a problem."

"Exactly! She doesn't deserve squat."

"She still has to pay the rent and the electricity, Mabel."

Mabel pouted. "If she needs money, why don't you just give it to her like a normal person?"

"She won't take it."

"Why not?"

"Because she doesn't want to admit she needs help, Mabel. Look, I know this is hard for you to understand because you're just a kid, but—"

"UGH!" Mabel screamed. "I am NOT *just a kid*!"

"I'm sorry. That's not what I meant. Look, I know this is hard. Mom's addiction to stealing things — you have to see it as a disease, not a character flaw."

"A disease?"

"Yes. I know that's hard to understand, but you have to know that she doesn't *want* to steal things, not exactly. It's like an uncontrollable urge... It's a mental illness, okay? The point is, we can't cure her. She has to change on her own — with a doctor or someone to help her, someone that knows what they're doing. So, the least we can do is show her some grace."

Mabel looked out the window and clenched her jaw, trying not to cry. She hated crying.

And, at this moment, she hated her mother. And she hated Sivaan for being nice to her.

"Mabel, listen to me. Families take care of each other. We stick together, even when we're not perfect."

"Is that what *she's* doing, Sivaan?" Mabel said with a shaky voice. "Is she taking care of us? Has she ever?"

"I don't expect you to understand right now, but, one day..." Sivaan let his voice trail off.

"I'll NEVER understand!" Mabel spat, and with that, she hopped out of the car, slammed the door behind her, and ran off into the woods.

NINE

Mabel was so distracted by her conversation with Sivaan that she practically forgot about the creepy encounter in Twyla's bedroom. She unlocked the front door with the porch key, let herself and Twyla inside, and robotically went to the kitchen to make a snack.

Mabel handed Twyla a plate of oatmeal creme pies and was about to take a seat on the couch when they both heard a voice drifting down the stairs.

"Wa-a-ant to pla-a-ay a ga-a-a-a-ame?"

Twyla's head turned slowly, knowingly.

"No," Mabel said, anticipating Twyla's request.

Twyla ignored Mabel and slid off the couch, setting the plate of cookies on the table.

"Absolutely not, Twyla," Mabel argued. "No going upstairs." She stood in Twyla's way.

"I want Bones," Twyla said firmly.

"Then ask Kristy later, but right now? No way. Bones stays up there and you stay down here. The end."

Twyla turned and went the other way to circumnavigate the table. Mabel took two steps to the side to block her from going any further.

"I'm going upstairs now," the little girl insisted.

"No!"

Twyla flashed her characteristically evil grin. "What are you going to do to stop me. Spank me?"

Mabel's blood ran cold. This kid....

Twyla walked past Mabel to the foot of the stairs. Mabel ran over and put her arm across the entry.

"Stop!" Mabel shouted.

Twyla leaned forward and bit Mabel's arm.

"Ow!" Mabel shrieked.

Twyla giggled and ran up the stairs into her room.

Fine, thought Mabel as she rubbed her arm. *Let the kid get eaten by her daddy closet monster.*

"Ga-a-ame. Ga-a-a-ame. Ga-a-a-a-ame," Bones's low voice muttered in a loop.

Mabel closed her eyes. What would Sivaan do? Call 911? They would never believe her. And they would probably take too long, if they were willing to go to Spite Lane at all.

Mabel realized that, if Twyla were in danger, she'd have to try to save her. It was her *job*. She was the babysitter. She was the one responsible for Twyla if anything happened.

Mabel *had* to go upstairs.

Slowly, Mabel dragged her feet up step by step. As she climbed the stairs, she heard noises like small animals scuttling around the room, and she saw the same yellow light from before growing brighter and brighter. There was an echo as Twyla devilishly giggled.

Mabel felt sweat roll down her cheek and she plastered her back to the wall outside Twyla's bedroom door. The yellow light began to flare and strobe. There was a squealing, scraping sound like something digging into the wood floor. Mabel peeked around the door frame over her shoulder.

As before, Twyla sat in bed. The closet door stood ajar. And everything in the room moved towards the closet as though pulled by an invisible force, like the closet had its own gravitational pull. The scraping noise was the sound of the bed legs gouging the wood as they dragged across the floor.

Mabel realized that, if she did nothing, the closet was going to swallow Twyla whole. And that couldn't be a good thing.

Mabel closed her eyes and began to count down. Three, two —

She leapt into the room, attempted to sprint towards Twyla, but sure enough, the room spun like a clothes dryer all around her. It was as though Twyla and her bed were above Mabel instead of ahead of her. Mabel turned and fell sideways, her forehead hitting the floor. Then, she started to slide towards the closet, too. At all of this, Twyla clapped and laughed.

Mabel reached out and desperately grasped Twyla's bed leg with the tips of her fingers. She held on for dear life. Kicking her legs up, she managed to get a foot over the end of the bed. She yanked as hard as she could, hooking the spindles at the foot of the bed with her elbow. Twyla screamed in fervent delight.

A clock radio from Twyla's bedside table whipped through the air and slammed against the wall next to the closet. It glowed in undulating colors as it played a warbled tune. Children sang, "Stay! Stay! Forever we stay! We promised not to go away!" Eerily, Twyla began to sing along.

As Twyla sang, the brilliant light emanating from the closet began to strobe faster and faster. Mabel could barely see, but she looked back over her shoulder anyway.

What she saw made her scream.

The opening to what had once been a closet was now a giant face — the demonic face of Bones — with a gaping maw that roared and sucked and tried to swallow them up.

"NO! LEAVE HER ALONE!" Mabel yelled. "Twyla, get out of here! RUN!"

But Twyla, seemingly immune to the supernatural forces, just laughed.

Mabel felt completely helpless. In seconds, they would both be dead.

Mabel's fingers were giving out and she was about to throw in the towel when Kristy Thomas appeared out of nowhere. She ran into the room and launched herself at the closet door, slamming it shut with a vicious roar.

The world instantly righted itself. Up was once again up, and down was once again down. Mabel crashed into the floor and rolled, wrapping herself up like a burrito in the bed sheets.

Ms. Thomas ran to Twyla and scooped her up, but Twyla began to kick and punch in protest. Although the closet door was shut, the light behind it still strobed, flashing against the wood floor, and flickering on Twyla's strained face.

"That's enough!" the woman yelled, trying to get a handle on the girl. "We have to get out of here, once and for all!"

"NOOO!" Twyla screamed, still flailing. "I want to stay! I want to be with Daddy! I want to stay in this house!"

As Kristy Thomas locked the girl in her grasp, she looked over at Mabel. "Go! Get out of here!"

Twyla protested, "STAY!"

The closet door began to groan. Mabel realized the wood panels were starting to bulge. The wood crackled as it started to split. Yellow light shone through the tiny fissures. She flexed her arms and legs, pushing herself free from the sheets.

"I hate you! You're not my mom!" screamed Twyla to Kristy. As if to accentuate her anger, there was a pounding that came from inside the closet. "You can't make us leave!"

The top panel of the door ruptured and yellow light poured through.

"STAY," commanded a voice in the closet. This time, Mabel knew it wasn't Bones, not really. It was something else. It was the voice of the haunted house itself.

Twyla squealed, "DADDY!"

"That's not your daddy!" Ms. Thomas yelled. "I don't know what that is, but it's not him!"

"STAY FOREVER," the voice boomed.

"Daddy! I want my daddy!"

All over again, the direction of gravity shifted. Mabel felt the room spin.

Kristy Thomas looked at Mabel and screamed, "GO!"

Before she was upsidedown once more, Mabel made a run for the staircase. She thought the woman and child were on her heels, but when she looked back at the bedroom, she saw they hadn't yet made it out the door.

There was a huge crack as the closet door gave way turning into a gaping, salivating mouth that violently sucked in everything around it. There would be no slamming it shut this time. Like a whirlpool, the force pulled Ms. Thomas and Twyla backwards into the room.

Mabel, with one hand on the bedroom door frame, reached for Ms. Thomas with the other.

"Grab my hand!" she yelled.

But taking Mabel's hand meant Kristy would have to take one hand off of Twyla. As soon as she did so, the little girl took advantage and wiggled herself out of the woman's grasp.

"Twyla, no! Please!" Kristy yelled. "Please — I love you! Don't do this! NO!"

As Twyla disappeared into the hungry mouth of the closet monster, Kristy Thomas screamed, "MY BABY!" She reached back for the missing girl in vain.

"Give me your other hand!" Mabel yelled at Ms. Thomas. "Hurry!"

But the woman looked at Mabel with resignation.

"I can't," she shouted over the din. "We're a family. We belong together."

She relaxed the hand holding Mabel's, let go, and vanished beyond the closet door.

The closet light went out and the door abruptly reassembled itself. Everything in the room fell in a heap to the floor. The world returned to normal.

And Mabel Mandal, dizzy and reeling, walked straight over to the stair railing and barfed.

Mabel sat on the floor of the hallway in a daze, not knowing how much time had passed, when she finally felt like her legs were solid enough to stand and she had gathered enough courage to look through the bedroom door.

There was nothing to see. Twyla's room looked undisturbed. Her bed was made. Stuffed animals crowded the toy basket. The closet door sat open only a crack, and no light shone inside. There was no evidence of what happened — and no sign of Twyla or Kristy.

Mabel didn't know what she was supposed to do. Should she have called 911? Would that have made a difference?

If she called them now, she worried she would be blamed for the family's disappearance. Could the police send a 13yo to jail for murder?

It isn't really murder if there aren't any dead bodies, Mabel thought, and she chuckled morbidly at the macabre thought.

Her eyes naturally wandered up to the ceiling. She gulped in horror at what she saw. In a repeating pattern were bucolic scenes of a happy family. A woman, a man, and a child were having a picnic. Altogether, they were swinging in a hammock. With the child in the middle, they were holding hands and going for a walk. They were laughing and playing hide-and-seek under a canopy of trees.

It wasn't just any family. It was clearly Twyla, Kristy, and what Mabel assumed was Twyla's father. They were frozen in their happily ever after — until they slowly turned to Mabel and winked — all of them, in every scene. Mabel screamed.

As the people in the wallpaper came to life across the room, Mabel heard a familiar voice coming from the closet.

"Are you ready for—"

Nope, she thought.

And Mabel ran.

TEN

When Sivaan picked up Mabel from the coffee shop a little while later, Mabel did her best to act as if nothing strange had happened that day. She didn't want to talk about it. She didn't know what to say. So Mabel just watched the pine trees blur by as they drove down Blue Angel Parkway. They passed shopping complexes and neighborhoods of cute clapboard houses. The farther they got from Spite Lane, the more unreal what had happened seemed, and Mabel started to question whether it had happened at all.

Still, Mabel was afraid of accidentally blurting out anything that might reveal what she *thought* had happened. Luckily, Sivaan didn't try to make small talk on the way home. Maybe he thought she was still angry after their argument earlier, or maybe he sensed her babysitting job hadn't gone well. Either way, the ride was silent and for that, Mabel was grateful.

When they got home, Mabel ran to her room and closed her bedroom door behind her. Her immediate instinct was to check her closet. It had unfinished birch wood folding doors that stood wide open. Inside was a shamble of boxes, clothes and old toys. No sign of any monsters. No strobing yellow lights. No toy trains with garishly large eyes and bulging mouths that begged for adventure.

Mabel scanned her bedroom walls. Her father had painted them a cheery blue when she was little. There had never been any wallpaper border. Posters of her favorite band and movies adorned the walls under softly blinking string lights. A giant bulletin board burst with family photos, birthday cards, and inspirational quotes. A mirror box with a thin glass shelf held a few trinkets she'd collected over the years: a vintage yo-yo, a carved ivory elephant, and a tea cup from a children's tea set she'd broken long ago.

Mabel sighed. There was nothing to be afraid of here. Nothing but herself.

From one back pocket, she pulled her phone and tossed it on the bed covers. From the other pocket, she pulled a wallet. She held it gingerly, running her fingers over the soft leather and decorative stitching, turning it over and over in her hands.

It wasn't just any wallet. And it wasn't Mabel's. It had belonged to Ms. Thomas.

Mabel had swiped it from the purse hanging on the hook by the door as she ran from the Thomas home.

She hadn't thought about it before she'd done it, she'd just grabbed it and run. Did that count as stealing? Mabel knew the answer. She'd swiped the woman's wallet, same as her mother swiped her brother's money from his sock drawer. It wasn't right. But... was it wrong?

Some part of her felt justified. After all, if the Thomas family hadn't been swallowed by the closet, Kristy would have paid her what she was owed. And she *was* owed....

Mabel unzipped Kristy's wallet. It was full of cash — the perfect amount with which to pay Mabel for Wednesday and Thursday. No more, no less. It wasn't really stealing. If the Thomas family were alive, she could always give it back.

As Mabel pulled it out, she realized there was also a small photo. It was a family portrait, the three of them smiling — Kristy, Twyla, and Twyla's dad. They looked happy — just like the images burned into the wallpaper border. Mabel whipped the wallet onto the floor as though it were a hot coal.

Just then, someone knocked. The door cracked open. It was Sivaan.

He stuck his face through the opening and said, "Hey, sorry to bother you."

"It's okay," Mabel said as she slid the cash under her butt.

Sivaan opened the door a little wider and stepped inside. "I just wanted to let you know that I can't give you a ride tomorrow. I was scheduled to take over someone else's shift. Do you think you could get a ride from someone else — or maybe take the bus?"

"It's okay," Mabel assured him. "I'm not going back."

"You're not? Everything okay?"

"Oh, totally," Mabel lied. "It's just that the kid is, uh, sick."

Sivaan nodded. Then he pointed at her bed with his chin. "What are you going to do with all that dough?"

Mabel frowned.

"Don't act like I don't know that trick," Sivaan laughed. "You hid a bunch of money under your butt as soon as I walked in. Don't worry, I'm not going to steal it."

Mabel blushed, caught. She glanced quickly to the side to make sure Ms. Thomas's wallet was out of Sivaan's line of sight, hidden just barely behind her clothes hamper. At least he didn't know about the wallet.

"I'm taking my friends out for Halloween. We're going to... see a movie."

Sivaan's shoulders loosened and a dopey smile spread across his face. "That's really generous of you, Mabel."

She smiled, but her belly burned with an acrid fire.

It's not generous if it's not your money to spend, a voice said in the back of Mabel's mind.

Sivaan turned to leave.

"Sivaan, wait," Mabel said, sliding the money out from under her. "Here, I owe you." She held out a five dollar bill.

Her older brother waved her off. "Don't worry about it," he said. "I'd just end up putting it back in my sock drawer, and then — well, you know what would happen. And I know you wouldn't approve."

Mabel chewed her lip before deciding what she wanted to say. "I think I kind of understand. About mom. I mean, I don't — but I want to."

Sivaan's giant brown eyes considered her as he said in a gentle tone, "Families take care of each other, right? I know it isn't conventional, but this is how I help take care of mom. And us."

Once again, Mabel didn't know what to say. With that, he left, and Mabel was all alone.

Later that evening, once Mabel was done with her homework, she realized she hadn't eaten since lunch. Her stomach growled at her to get a snack. On her way down the hall, she passed Sivaan's half-open door and caught a glimpse of him propped up yet asleep on his bed. Mabel's heart swelled with pride. He was a good brother — the best. He made her lunches and he drove her around. The least she could do was turn off his bedside lamp so he could get a good night's sleep.

As she approached, she saw he'd been reading a letter that now lie on his chest. That was odd. On closer look, Mabel was alarmed by the harsh words leaping from the page.

NOTICE OF TERMINATION, it said at the top. Further down, it read, YOU MUST VACATE THE PREMISES, and there was a date.

Mabel quickly scanned the document. She didn't understand all of it, but she got the gist. Their lease was being terminated for non-payment.

They were being kicked out of their house — unless they caught up on their rent.

They had less than 30 days.

No wonder Sivaan had been so willing to help their mom with money. Things were far worse than Mabel could have ever imagined.

Fear coursed through Mabel's veins. It was a very different kind of fear than the kind she'd experienced at the Thomas house on Spite Lane. This time, the monster wasn't after her, it was after her family.

Mabel silently flipped off Sivaan's lamp and slinked back to her own room, her appetite non-existent. There had to be something she could do.

Her mind was swirling as she walked over to the shelf and grabbed the piggy bank. She slipped off the false bottom and studied the money folded there. She was so confused. She just wanted to go to Torture Town with her friends and have some fun. And she didn't want to help her mom — Katie was the one that had gotten them into this mess.

But she wanted to help Sivaan. And she didn't want them to have to move out.

Mabel grabbed the folded stack of bills and carried it to Sivaan's room where she silently stuffed it into his sock drawer. Then she went back to her room and crawled under the covers of her bed and squeezed her eyes shut. Her mind buzzed, her ears rung, and her heart felt like it might beat straight out of her chest.

Now she had nothing to pay for tickets to Torture Town. What was she going to tell her friends?

As Mabel drifted off to sleep, she kept hearing Bones's voice as though the possessed toy were whispering in her ear: "We're running out of time. We're running out of time."

Eleven

All day Thursday, Mabel had done her best to pretend that nothing was wrong. She didn't have the heart to tell her friends what she'd done — that she didn't have enough money to take them all to Torture Town.

When Mabel's alarm wailed to life early Friday morning, the first thought that leapt to the front of Mabel's consciousness was, *Halloween is ruined, and it's all my fault.*

At lunch, Fernanda told everyone to be ready by 5 for their ride to the county fairgrounds where the haunted house was the main seasonal attraction. Mabel thought this was it, her chance to say, sorry, I can't get us tickets to Torture Town after all. But then everyone would ask what happened to the money, and Mabel didn't want to have to tell them the truth: she'd felt so guilty about stealing from the Thomas family after they'd been swallowed by their own house that she'd hidden the money in her brother's room for her mom to steal.

Sure, it was the truth, but what an awful truth to reveal.

By the time Friday evening had arrived, Mabel was a bundle of nerves. The truth was going to come out one way or the other.

Mabel was basically hiding in her room when, right on cue, she heard the doorbell ring. A moment later, Sivaan knocked on her bedroom door.

"Your friends are here," he said without opening it and walked away.

Mabel didn't know how she was going to explain things. She steeled herself as she went downstairs to meet them.

Asher and Suki stood on her front steps wearing their costumes. Fernanda stood behind them, head bowed over her phone, face aglow. Mabel took a deep breath and stepped outside, closing the front door softly behind her.

"You're not dressed!" Suki exclaimed with disappointment.

"Right... about that..." Mabel hoped they couldn't see how puffy her eyes were from crying. "Um, it turns out I don't have enough money to get tickets to Torture Town for everyone after all."

"What?!" Archer and Suki shrieked. Fernanda briefly looked up from her phone, but only for a second.

"I know, I know, I'm sorry, it's just, um, uh, I just —"

"What happened?" Archer demanded.

Mabel opened and closed her mouth, but nothing came out.

"Girl, you can't be serious," Archer chided. "You've been acting weird all week. I knew something was up."

Mabel felt like she had a whole apple stuck in her throat. "I forgot I owed Sivaan," she croaked.

"Dang, girl, you owed him that much money?" Archer chided, shaking his head in disappointment. "Oh, well. I knew it was too good to be true."

"What are we going to do now?" Suki wailed. She tugged at the electric blue piggy tails of her wig.

"I don't know," Mabel answered. "I guess we could just go trick-or-treating..."

"We are WAY too old for that nonsense," Archer spat.

"We're going to Torture Town," Fernanda murmured into her chest, so low, they almost didn't hear her.

"What?" Archer asked, turning.

Fernanda held up her phone. "I got tickets. We can still go."

"Seriously?" Mabel's mouth fell open in disbelief. "You just bought tickets right now?"

"Yeah," Fernanda said. "Online. It was easy."

"Fernanda — I — uh — thank you," Mabel stuttered. "I don't know what else to say. I guess I owe you."

"Yeah. You can pay me back later," Fernanda said. "My mom's waiting in the car, so we should go now."

Suki and Archer went from crestfallen to jumping up and down for joy. "Torture Town! Torture Town! Torture Town!" they chanted and ran to Fernanda's mom's car.

The teens climbed into the large, black SUV that sat idling at the end of the driveway, but Mabel stopped to look back at her house one more time.

She should have been excited — the night wasn't ruined after all.

So why did she still feel so awful?

She squished into the backseat next to her friends, and the SUV sped off down the street towards the scariest haunted house in town.

Torture Town stood at the far end of the county fairgrounds, past a field of tall grass that created a border against the carnival rides set up for families with young kids. Mabel and her friends pushed their way through screaming devils, cackling witches, and shrieking vampires running amok of frenzied parents to get to the main event.

Walking up to the enormous metal warehouse that had been converted to a haunted house, Mabel thought how cartoonish it looked compared to the houses on Spite Lane. Four tall animatronic skeletons loomed over the entrance. Ragged tendrils of burlap sack cloth hung from the roof as well as the arms of the boney beasts. Speakers played creepy organ music, and a smoke machine piped out a fog that obscured the dirt ground.

"This is so cool!" Suki squealed under red and purple lights that swirled all around them.

But Mabel was unimpressed. Everything looked so... fake. She tried to psych herself up. Hopefully it would feel much scarier once they got inside.

The lengthy line of attendees moved slowly as groups were staggered for entry in batches of two to four. While they waited, Fernanda handed everyone their fake IDs. Mabel hadn't put on her costume or makeup, so Suki pulled a dark lipstick out of her purse and told Mabel to put it on while she held up a mirrored compact so Mabel could see. She hoped they would be able to pass for at least 16.

But the older teen at the door (Mabel guessed he was Sivaan's age) barely glanced at their fake driver's licenses as he waited for the call over his walkie talkie to tell him it was their turn. When the call came through, he shooed them forward with a bored sigh.

"Let's go!" Archer shouted as they held hands and ran through the black curtained entrance.

Mabel couldn't see a thing at first. Once they were beyond the curtains, they were thrust into pitch blackness. The four of them stopped with Archer and Suki on each end feeling around with their free hands.

"I think there's a door," said Suki, and they inched their way towards an opening.

A light began to flicker, then steadily glow. It illuminated a small room that had been decorated like the foyer of a haunted mansion. Candelabras sat upon dusty tables surrounded by random odds and ends: a skull, a rubber rat, a bunch of plastic spiders, and cotton stretched thin to form cobwebs. Mabel couldn't contain her disappointment.

"Oh, come on," she muttered, letting go of Fernanda's and Archer's hands.

They inspected the room, all turned in different directions. Suki leaned in to take a closer look at a Gothic painting of a pale man in a black suit when it abruptly came to life. The man roared and reached for her as he leaned out of the painting. Suki shrieked and ran. Archer and Fernanda yelled and ran, too, with Mabel at the rear.

They passed through room after room of disturbing scenes under strobing lights. There was a child's bedroom full of creepy toys. The child (a haunted house employee in costume) sat up in bed and hands shot out from under it to grab their ankles. There was an operating room with a grotesque surgical scene. The patient vomited and gagged. In the dungeon, bodies hung from the ceiling wrapped in ropes and chains. Some of them tried to grab Mabel and her friends.

It was exciting, but Mabel wasn't actually scared. It wasn't real. Not like the house on Spite Lane.

The halls twisted and turned from room to room and scene to scene. The teens did their best to stick together, but their adrenaline was running high when Mabel, still holding up the rear, felt her hoodie catch on something. Her friends ran ahead around a corner. She lost sight of them as she tried to figure out what she was caught on and get free.

As soon as she felt the hoodie loosen, she was thrust into complete darkness once again. She couldn't see a thing. Mabel felt in front of her as she walked, trying to find the corner her friends had turned. Her hands hit something soft.

A person.

Hair.

She pulled back and stopped.

"Hello?" Mabel said. Her voice disappeared into the void.

A light appeared, faint, from overhead, and in front of her, she saw the thing she had touched.

It was a girl, about six.

Her long stringy hair hung down over her shoulders.

Her eyes were as blank as her expression.

But it wasn't just any girl.

It was Twyla.

"No," Mabel whispered. "No, no, no."

Twyla took a step forward and smiled. Her eye sockets were black, empty. When her lips parted in a grin, her teeth were sharp, like little points.

"Not real," Mabel said. "You're not real."

"You shouldn't have left," Twyla gurgled as tendrils of blood dripped from the corners of her mouth. "Don't leave me again. Please? Ple-e-e-e-ease?"

Twyla put out a hand, but Mabel just looked at it. Guilt swelled inside of her chest, and a sob caught in her throat. Was it true? Was what happened to Twyla her fault?

The little girl dragged her feet closer to Mabel. That's when Mabel smelled something foul, something like rotten meat. As the girl continued to plead, the smell became stronger. Death floated out of Twyla's mouth. Mabel could taste it on her tongue. She tried not to retch.

Conflicted, she pushed past Twyla and ran into the shadows, hoping not to run into a wall. She ran and ran until it felt like she'd run around an entire city block. She hit a barrier made out of fabric and felt it wrap around her like a sack.

Losing her footing, Mabel fell. She pulled at the velvet tapestry that covered her face and looked up to see she was just outside the exit to the warehouse. Her friends stood in a row with perplexed expressions on their faces.

"Mabel, are you okay?" Fernanda asked with more concern than Mabel had ever heard from her.

Mabel dusted herself off as she stood. "Yeah. I'm fine."

"That. Was. AMAZING!" Suki screeched, hopping up and down with glee. "I wish we could do it again!"

"Look," said Fernanda. She was pointing to one of the television monitors that was posted outside a booth by the exit. They were selling photos of the attendees as they had run screaming through the haunted house. On the monitor, Mabel saw herself, alone, and her face, her mouth open in surprise. There was no sign of the ghastly girl.

"Mabel, you legit look like you saw a ghost!" said Archer, laughing.

Mabel couldn't take it. She was about to spill her guts, tell them everything that had happened at the Thomas house and what she'd seen inside that hall, when Suki interrupted.

"Ohmigod, that's all of us!" she yelled as another picture cycled through, this one of Suki, Archer and Fernanda all screaming and holding onto each other for dear life.

"Best night ever!" Archer announced, and with that, they headed back to the family friendly side of the fairgrounds where Archer bought some cotton candy and shared it with his friends.

Mabel, still in shock, kept her mouth shut about what she'd seen.

When Mabel got home later that evening, she collapsed onto her bed in exhaustion. She didn't know what had taken more energy: running from Twyla's ghost or pretending to have a good time with her friends.

She'd been haunted by Twyla's ghost. It had happened. Mabel had felt her hair. She was really there. She was real.

Wasn't she?

Maybe it was just a figment of her imagination. Maybe it was just some kid dressed up for the haunted house and Mabel's mind had tricked her into thinking it was Twyla.

Mabel grabbed the laptop from the end of her bed, planning to research hauntings, when she saw there were twelve new Facebook message notifications! Mabel began to scroll through them, elated to realize each was an offer for a new babysitting gig.

But the news wasn't all good. The requests had come from Spite Lane — every single one of them.

No way she was going back there. She had already survived enough hauntings for one week!

But...

She owed Fernanda money. Sivaan needed help, too. Realistically, it made no sense to turn down these jobs.

Mabel took a closer look, reading through the details. Like Kristy Thomas, they were offering premium pay. After all, who else would dare babysit on Spite Lane but Mabel Mandal?

However, some of them requested the same dates and times. Mabel couldn't take all twelve jobs — not without some help.

Her phone buzzed. A serendipitous text from Archer appeared.

HARRY STYLES TICKETS GO ON SALE NEXT WEEK!!!! ANY CHANCE YOU NEED HELP BABYSITTING?

Mabel, she told herself, *don't be an idiot! Do NOT take any of these jobs because they are on Spite Lane, and Spite Lane is H-A-U-N-T-E-D!*

But what she typed back to Asher was, FUNNY YOU SHOULD ASK...

For $30 an hour, maybe a few haunted houses weren't the end of the world. After all, she'd survived the first babysitting gig.

But who knew what the other houses had in store. And how could she be sure she could keep herself or her friends safe?

Mabel turned the offers over in her mind, deciding she would reply to the messages and tell them she would love to babysit any time. She was going to have to decide whether to tell Archer what had happened to Twyla. Perhaps they could come up with a plan to prevent any more supernatural shenanigans. Maybe they could even figure out a way to get the Thomas family back.

Mabel was determined to be the best babysitter ever, despite what had happened to Twyla and what Mrs. Grace had said. She wasn't sure how she was going to do it... but there was only one way to find out.

Mabel Mandal was going back to Spite Lane.

ACKNOWLEDGEMENTS

Acknowledgements

It takes a village to make a book series, and mine is full of so many wonderful people.

First, I have to thank author Sarah Dinan for inspiring me to write this book series. I am so lucky to work with you.

I am also so very grateful for my husband, David. Thank you for always betting on me. You are always and forever my favorite.

Thank you to my Instagram community for supporting me and being as excited about this series launch as I was.

Last but not least, thank you to my readers for supporting indie authors. It means the world to us. I can't wait to join you in Lost Key again soon.

ABOUT THE AUTHOR

About the Author

Christiane Erwin is the author of JUDE'S DIARY, a supernatural thriller about one teenager willing to do whatever it takes to get what she wants, and THE SPITE LANE HAUNTINGS series which include THE VOICE IN THE CLOSET, THE BEE KEEPER'S SON, and THE BABY CRIES AFTER MIDNIGHT. When she's not writing, you can find her fostering dogs, rock climbing, and spending time with her human and fur family in Marietta, Georgia.

Also by Christiane Erwin

THE SPITE LANE HAUNTINGS

Printed in Great Britain
by Amazon

39482152R00076